INSECTS: SIX-LEGGED NIGHTMARES

BULLET ANTS STING!

BY MELISSA RAÉ SHOFNER

Gareth Stevens
PUBLISHING

Please visit our website, www.garethstevens.com. For a free color catalog of all our high-quality books, call toll free 1-800-542-2595 or fax 1-877-542-2596.

Cataloging-in-Publication Data

Names: Shofner, Melissa Raé.
Title: Bullet ants sting! / Melissa Raé Shofner.
Description: New York : Gareth Stevens Publishing, 2018. | Series: Insects: six-legged nightmares | Includes index.
Identifiers: ISBN 9781538212554 (pbk.) | ISBN 9781538212578 (library bound) | ISBN 9781538212561 (6 pack)
Subjects: LCSH: Ants–Juvenile literature.
Classification: LCC QL568.F7 S56 2018 | DDC 595.79'6–dc23

First Edition

Published in 2018 by
Gareth Stevens Publishing
111 East 14th Street, Suite 349
New York, NY 10003

Designer: Laura Bowen
Editor: Ryan Nagelhout/Kate Mikoley

Photo credits: Cover, p. 1 (bullet ant) Dr Morley Read/Stockbyte/Getty Images; cover, pp. 1–24 (background) Fantom666/Shutterstock.com; cover, pp. 1–24 (black splatter) Miloje/Shutterstock.com; cover, pp. 1–24 (web) Ramona Kaulitzki/Shutterstock.com; pp. 4–24 (text boxes) Tueris/Shutterstock.com; p. 5 (fire ant) boyphare/Shutterstock.com; p. 5 (army ant) Dr Morley Read/Shutterstock.com; p. 5 (bullet ant) Hugh Lansdown/Shutterstock.com; p. 7 Archaeodontosaurus/WIkimedia Commons; pp. 9 (ant), 17 (velvet ant) Josve05a/Wikimedia Commons; p. 11 Cyril Ruoso/Minden Pictures/Getty Images; p. 13 Aldo Brando/Oxford Scientific/Getty Images; p. 15 Piotr Naskrecki/Minden Pictures/Getty Images; p. 17 (bee) VBuhl/Wikimedia Commons; p. 17 (Asian giant hornet) File Upload Bot (Magnus Manske)/Wikimedia Commons; p. 17 (bullet ant) The Photographer/Wikimedia Commons; p. 19 De Agostini Picture Library/Getty Images; p. 21 Mark Bowler/Science Source/Getty Images.

Printed in China

CPSIA compliance information: Batch #CW18GS: For further information contact Gareth Stevens, New York, New York at 1-800-542-2595.

CONTENTS

Words in the glossary appear in **bold** type the first time they are used in the text.

AWESOME ANTS!

Ants are really cool creatures. They're small but strong, and they use teamwork to get things done. They're found around the world in all sorts of places, including deserts, mountains, and rainforests.

There may be as many as 14,000 species, or kinds, of ants, and some are pretty scary. Army ants will destroy any plants or small animals that get in their way. Bullet ants, however, are truly terrifying. They're the largest species of ant, and they're best known for their unbelievably painful sting!

TERRIFYING TRUTHS

Fire ants have a sting that feels like being burned by a flame. Bullet ants, however, have a sting that feels like being shot by a gun!

fire ant

army ant

bullet ant

Bullet ants look a lot like ants you might see marching down the sidewalk, but they're much bigger and can cause a lot of pain!

ANTS ARE INSECTS

Like other ants, bullet ants are insects. Insects have six legs and three body sections, or parts: a head, thorax, and abdomen. Ants have antennae on their head, which they use to sense things around them. They also have strong **jaws**.

An ant's legs are joined to its thorax, or middle section. Some ants may also have wings on their thorax. An ant's stomach is found in its rear section, which is called the abdomen. Ants also have a hard outer covering called an exoskeleton.

TERRIFYING TRUTHS

Bullet ants are reddish-black and may look sort of hairy. They can grow up to 1.2 inches (3 cm) long!

PARTS OF A BULLET ANT

Watch out for the stinger on a bullet ant's abdomen. It's sharp and has strong **venom**!

TROPICAL TERRORS

Bullet ants live in Central and South America. Their range reaches across several countries, from Honduras down to Paraguay and over into Brazil. You won't find bullet ants anywhere outside of Central and South America.

Bullet ants are usually found in rainforests. Rainforests are tropical areas, which means they're hot, wet, and full of plants. Bullet ants live in nests, which are often built near the base of a tree. Some nests reach up to 2 feet (0.6 m) below the ground.

TERRIFYING TRUTHS

Bullet ants may also make their nests at the base of other plants such as tropical bushes and **vines**.

BULLET ANT RANGE MAP

You may not have heard about bullet ants before reading this book, but people in Central and South America are very aware of these ants and their painful sting!

THE QUEEN AND HER COLONY

Ants live in large groups called colonies. Bullet ant colonies may have between a few hundred and 1,000 members. Their colonies are small compared to those of some other ant species.

Each colony has a single queen and many workers. The queen ant's job is to lay eggs. Worker ants have several important jobs within a colony. They climb high into the trees to find food. They also **protect** the colony and help care for the young.

TERRIFYING TRUTHS

Bullet ant colonies are independent and don't **interact** with each other.

Some worker bullet ants stay near the ground and guard the nest entrances.

BABY BULLET ANTS

To start a colony, a queen ant must **mate**. She then lays the eggs. These eggs will soon hatch into larvae, which look like little white worms. Larvae molt, or shed their skin, several times as they grow.

Bullet ant larvae enter the pupa stage once they've grown big enough. During this stage, ants will change into their adult form. Most pupae will become workers. An ant's life cycle—egg to larva to pupa to adult—takes about 6 to 10 weeks.

TERRIFYING TRUTHS

The scientific name for bullet ants is *Paraponera clavata*. Their closest known **relative**, *Paraponera dieteri*, died out millions of years ago.

Sometimes worker ants carry larvae in their jaws.

FORAGING FOR FOOD

Bullet ant workers are in charge of finding food for their colony. They climb up into the trees where they forage, or search for food. Bullet ants like to eat small insects such as crickets, termites, and flies. They'll also eat insect larvae, including mealworms and wax worms.

Nectar and sap are a bullet ant's favorite foods. They use their jaws to carry small bits of food back to the nest where the colony eats.

TERRIFYING TRUTHS

Bullet ants place small pieces of food onto their larvae to feed them.

Bullet ants don't hunt in groups. Individuals search for food on their own.

bullet ant with caterpillar

OUCH!

Bullet ants have the most painful sting of any insect. But their stinger is only 0.04 to 0.12 inch (1 to 3 mm) long! When a bullet ant stings a person or other animal, its venom is passed to them. Bullet ant venom is a neurotoxin. Neurotoxins are poisons that attack **nerve** cells, which can cause **paralysis**.

Bullet ant venom isn't deadly for people, but it does cause unbelievable pain. Multiple stings can cause shaking and short-term paralysis. Luckily, bullet ants aren't usually **aggressive**. If you don't bother them, they should leave you alone.

TERRIFYING TRUTHS

Before stinging, a bullet ant will give off a strong odor. Those who don't pay attention to this warning might receive a painful sting!

SCHMIDT STING PAIN INDEX

This system rates the pain caused by different insect stings and bites on a scale of 1 to 4. With a 4+ rating, the bullet ant sting tops the list! The scientist who created this scale was bitten and stung many times while figuring out the rankings.

1 BEE

2 ASIAN GIANT HORNET

3 VELVET ANT

4+ BULLET ANT

RITE OF PASSAGE

The Satere-Mawe people of the Amazon rainforest have an interesting connection with bullet ants. Before young boys become warriors, or fighters, they often wear special gloves filled with these stinging ants.

Hundreds of bullet ants are carefully collected and placed into large basketlike gloves. Boys who are ready to take part in this act place their hands into the gloves. The angry ants give many painful stings while the boys dance and sing for 10 minutes.

TERRIFYING TRUTHS

Young Satere-Mawe boys may wear the bullet ant gloves many times over several months or years before they're considered warriors.

The hands and arms of the young Satere-Mawe boys may swell up, shake uncontrollably, or become briefly paralyzed. The act of being stung is meant to teach the boys that suffering and effort are important parts of life.

HANDLED BY HUMANS

The Satere-Mawes and the creator of the pain scale aren't the only people who handle bullet ants. Some scientists work very closely with the ants to learn more about them. These people are highly trained at working with dangerous insects and use their findings to help others.

Surprisingly, bullet ants may be able to help people with some kinds of illnesses. Scientists are studying bullet ants' neurotoxin to see how it may possibly be used to treat pain—instead of just causing it!

TERRIFYING TRUTHS

Bullet ants are also called "24-hour ants" because the pain caused by their venomous sting may last for 24 hours.

Bullet ant stings are sometimes used to treat **rheumatism**. The ants' strong jaws may be used to hold wounds closed, too.

GLOSSARY

aggressive: showing a readiness to attack

interact: to come together and have an effect on each other

jaws: the walls of the mouth

mate: to come together to make babies

nerve: a part of the body that sends messages to the brain and allows an animal to feel things

paralysis: the state of being unable to move

protect: to keep safe

relative: someone who belongs to the same group or family as someone else because of shared features

rheumatism: a medical condition involving pain in the muscles or joints

venom: something an animal makes in its body that can harm other animals

vine: a plant with a long stem that grows along the ground or up and around something else

FOR MORE INFORMATION

BOOKS

Hamilton, S. L. *Ants.* Minneapolis, MN: A & D Xtreme, 2015.

Simon, Seymour. *Deadly Ants.* Mineola, NY: Dover Publications, 2012.

Stewart, Amy. *Wicked Bugs: The Meanest, Deadliest, Grossest Bugs on Earth.* Chapel Hill, NC: Algonquin Young Readers, 2017.

WEBSITES

5 Spine-Chilling Facts About the Bullet Ant
www.fascinatingplanet.com/5-spine-chilling-facts-about-the-bullet-ant/
Visit this website for some frightening facts about bullet ants.

Bullet Ant Facts
www.activewild.com/bullet-ant-facts/
Find fascinating facts and videos about bullet ants here.

Bullet Ant Facts
animalstime.com/bullet-ant-facts/
Read more about bullet ants on this site.

Publisher's note to educators and parents: Our editors have carefully reviewed these websites to ensure that they are suitable for students. Many websites change frequently, however, and we cannot guarantee that a site's future contents will continue to meet our high standards of quality and educational value. Be advised that students should be closely supervised whenever they access the Internet.

INDEX